ZONE 13

They Came from the Sea

DAVID ORME

Ransom

They Came from the Sea
by David Orme
Illustrated by Jorge Mongiovi and Ulises Carpintero
Cover photograph: © slobo

Published by Ransom Publishing Ltd.
Radley House, 8 St. Cross Road, Winchester, Hampshire, SO23 9HX, UK
www.ransom.co.uk

ISBN   978 184167 457 5

First published in 2011
Reprinted 2013

Originally published in 1998 by Stanley Thornes Publishers Ltd.

A CIP catalogue record of this book is available from the British Library.

CONTENTS

THE LEAK

Rob Smart was the manager of a power station. He was worried. Six people had the flu. They were important people. It would be difficult to run the station without them.

Rob sat at the control desk. The only other person there was John. He was learning the job. Rob was the only person who knew what to do.

Rob rang the company that owned the power station.

'We have to shut down,' he said. 'It isn't safe to keep a nuclear power station working without trained people.'

The company boss did not agree to this.

'It is winter. Everybody needs electricity. We can't afford to shut down the station. If you can't do it, we'll find a new manager ...'

Rob put down the phone. He didn't feel very well either. 'I've got the flu too,' he thought. 'But I've got to carry on.'

Rob had been on duty for 24 hours. He felt sleepy. His eyes were closing ...

He woke up suddenly. The alarm was ringing!

Rob rushed to the control board. John was looking scared.

'I didn't know what to do. The reactor seems to be in trouble.'

Rob started to press switches. The alarm stopped.

'Why didn't you wake me?' he shouted. 'That reactor has been leaking!'

'Is it safe now?'

'Yes. The reactor won't melt down. But the cooling liquid has gone down the pipe to the sea!'

'Is that bad?'

'Of course it is. It's very radioactive! If anyone finds out, we are out of a job. Don't say anything about this!'

NOT FOR THE PUBLIC TO KNOW
TOP SECRET
ZONE 13 FILES ONLY

FIVE YEARS LATER

South Bay was a small seaside town. It had a sandy beach and hotels. There was a little harbour. Fishing boats went out to catch crabs and other seafood. The nuclear power station was on a hill behind the town.

Old Sid was worried. He was a fisherman. He caught crabs and fish. There were not many crabs these days. Those he did catch seemed very strange. He looked at one in the bottom of the boat. It had extra legs and claws.

A young woman was walking by the boat. She called to Sid.

'Can I come and speak to you?'

'Who are you?'

'My name's Jenny. I work for a group called Greensave. We are worried about pollution.'

Sid showed Jenny the crab.

'Could pollution make a crab grow extra legs?'

Jenny looked at the crab. She took out a machine and held it near to the crab. The machine made clicking noises.

'It's radioactive! Where did you catch this?'

'Out by Gull Rock.'

'That's where the power station waste pipe is!'

Old Sid nodded.

'Can I come out with you, next time you go fishing?' asked Jenny.

'You're very welcome.'

That afternoon Sid took Jenny out in his
boat. He showed her Gull Rock.

Suddenly they saw something in the water.
There was a splashing noise. A huge grey
head appeared. It opened its mouth. Jenny
and Sid saw rows of teeth.

The boat started rocking. At the same time, they heard a noise.

Something was trying to chew a hole in the bottom of the boat!

NOT FOR THE PUBLIC TO KNOW

TOP SECRET

ZONE 13 FILES ONLY

GULL ROCK

Water started coming in. Sid knew that they couldn't get back to land. He started the engine. He steered the boat towards Gull Rock.

'Quick, get out on to the rock! The boat is sinking!'

Jenny got out. Sid followed her. They watched the boat sink.

More grey heads showed in the water. They looked like seals, but their heads were too big. Their mouths were full of sharp teeth.

The seals crowded round the rock. They tried to climb out of the water. The rocks were too steep for them. Again and again they tried to get at the two people on the rocks.

'I've never seen seals like that!' said Sid. 'Look at the size of them!'

Then Sid remembered what time it was.

'The tide's coming in,' he said. 'The rock will be covered. Unless a boat comes past, we've had it!'

'We'll be all right,' said Jenny. 'I can call the coastguard on my mobile.'

Ten minutes later they heard the roar of an engine. It was a lifeboat!

The grey-headed creatures went away at the sound of the engine. Sid and Jenny were soon taken off the rock.

The lifeboat men didn't believe the story. They thought Sid must have hit the rocks.

'You fishermen do tell tales!' they said.

That evening, Jenny met Sid in a pub down by the beach.

'I'm sorry you lost your boat. What are you going to do now?'

'I'm not sorry,' said Sid. 'I will get the insurance money and retire.'

Just then they heard the sound of sirens.

Everyone rushed out of the pub. There was a police car and an ambulance by the beach.

Later, a man came into the pub. He looked pale.

'I called the police. I found two bodies on the beach. They were divers. There wasn't much left of them. They had been eaten!'

OUT OF THE SEA

The next day was hot and sunny. The beach was full of people. Some of them were swimming in the sea.

Jenny walked along the path at the top of the beach. She was sure that radiation was the problem. Seals were usually harmless.

Greensave had found out that there had been a leak from the power station. All the life in the sea near the waste pipe had been affected.

Suddenly there was a yell from the beach. People were standing up. They moved towards the water.

'Seals!' someone said. 'Look at the seals!'

Big grey heads were looking out of the water. People were excited. They were walking into the sea towards them.

Jenny ran down to the beach,

'Get out of the water,' she yelled. 'They're dangerous!'

People laughed. 'They're just seals!'

The seals attacked together. People ran out of the water. They were screaming. Most of them got back to the beach.

Some didn't.
The sea turned red with blood.

5

THE COVER-UP

By midday, the army had arrived. The beach was closed. Navy ships stopped boats at sea. A search of the coast began. One by one, the dangerous seals were found and killed.

'The seals went mad. It was caused by a virus,' said the government.

They didn't mention the waste pipe from the power station. Jenny knew that the government was covering up the real reason.

Jenny went to call on Sid. He lived in a little cottage by the harbour.

'The radioactive waste got into the food chain,' she told Sid. 'First it went into the tiny creatures. The fish ate them. Then the seals ate the fish. The seals must have been affected before they were born. The killer seals were starving because they had eaten all the fish.'

Just then Sid's daughter came in. Jenny saw that she was about to have a baby.

Sid smiled at her. 'This is Laura,' he told Jenny. 'I'm about to have my first grandchild.'

'I heard that you are retiring,' said Laura to her dad. 'That's a pity. The fish you have been bringing have been so good. And what a size they were! I've hardly eaten anything else for months.'

Sid looked at his daughter.

He thought about what Jenny had just said –

'The killer seals must have been affected before they were born.'

Sid stopped smiling.

Suddenly his face was full of fear.

NOT FOR THE PUBLIC TO KNOW
TOP SECRET
ZONE 13 FILES ONLY

ABOUT THE AUTHOR

David Orme is an expert on strange, unexplained events. For his protection (and yours) we cannot show a photograph of him.

David created the Zone 13 files to record the cases he studied. Some of these files really do involve aliens, but many do not. Aliens are not everywhere. Just in most places.

These stories are all taken from the Zone 13 files. They will not be here for long. Read them while you can.

But don't close your eyes when you go to sleep at night. **They** will be watching you.